SCARY TALES FOR NAUGHTY KIDS

Marcelina Kosińska

Self-translated text with the help of a translator.
ISBN: 978-83-67375-03-0

CONTENTS

SCARY TALES FOR NAUGHTY KIDS

1. The Prince and the Vampire

Once upon a time, beyond the mountains, beyond the forests, there was a beautiful kingdom. It was ruled by a righteous king who had only one child. He was a son, unusually handsome and brave, who was to take over from his wonderful father.

However, the teachings were not in the prince's mind. He went hunting and often went on adventurous journeys. The king was worried that his son did not want to settle down, marry a beautiful princess and sit on the throne.

One day the good ruler could not stand the prince's antics and said to him:
"Either you find a wife by the end of the year, or I won't give you the crown!"

The prince was very taken up by this and immediately began his search. It was not an easy task as none of the ladies suited him. Ultimately, the prince decided to find a mate in a neighboring kingdom. He set out on a journey through the forbidden forest. No one was allowed to approach this forest, because it was swarming with all kinds of spooks and ghouls. The prince was not afraid of anything and, with his head held high, he entered inaccessible areas.

It was a very dark place. The sun's rays did not reach here, and it was dark and damp everywhere. The prince rode his horse for a long time until he reached the old castle. He was surprised because he had not heard of any king ruling in this region. The building looked like a ruin. All the bricks were overgrown with moss, and there were no panes in the windows. The door, however, was closed, so the prince decided to knock. A beautiful princess opened him and the prince immediately fell in love with her. The beauty invited him inside and offered him a meal. Apart from her, there was no living soul in the entire castle.

- How is it possible that such a young and beautiful princess lives alone? The Prince wondered.

Despite many doubts, he decided that she would become his wife. The girl, however, did not want them to go to his kingdom during the day. She said her delicate skin reacts badly to the sun. So they decided to leave after sunset.

When the princess went for an afternoon nap, the prince began exploring the castle. He didn't meet any other people at all. He looked into many chambers and noticed that a lot of people must have lived here once, because each room was fully equipped and the personal belongings of former residents were on the tables. The prince looked at the portraits hanging in the corridors. He was surprised that none of them showed his heart.

Suddenly, standing in the dark corridor, he felt a chill. Straight ahead, a few meters away, he saw the silhouette of a woman. The white figure stood motionless and caused fear in the young man's heart. She wasn't moving, and in the dark it was hard to see the features of her face. The prince felt that she was looking directly at him.

- Who's there? He said hesitantly towards the phantom "is it you, my love?"

- Yes, it's me. Come to me - he heard a voice coming from the figure.

He walked uncertainly towards her. She still hadn't moved a bit. The farther he walked, the darker it seemed to get around.

When he was very close to the princess, she moved and stretched out both her hands towards him. The prince was terrified, because here in front of him, instead of a beautiful princess, stood a pale figure with red eyes. From the features of her face, she resembled his beloved, but it was obvious that she was not the same person. The young man was afraid to move. The woman approached and the prince's eyes saw sharp fangs, which he felt on his neck after a while. The apparition slowly drank all the blood that was flowing in its veins. He slumped gently to the floor, never to get up again. The apparition dissolved into thin air.

The king worried about his son and waited for his return for years. This one, however, never returned, and various legends were heard among the inhabitants of the kingdom. One of them told about a neighboring kingdom that took in a lost, beautiful girl. She turned out to be a ruthless vampire who drank the blood of all her saviors. After she had killed everyone, a very dense forest grew around the castle. However, no one knew where this place was.

2. A secret room

Once upon a time, in a small town, there lived a beautiful girl. She lived in a small house with her mother and three brothers. They never had enough money, so each member of the family tried to earn a few pennies by doing various activities. Everyone has worked hard.

Only the girl did not care about their situation. She did not help with the house, did not clean up after herself, and did not listen to the adults. On top of that, she was still rude and didn't talk nicely. The mother was very tired of this, and after many attempts to restore order, she said to her daughter:

- Beloved child. I work hard day and night. I am still tired. I don't like your behavior and I can't deal with you. I have decided that you will live with your uncle, at the other end of the kingdom.

After these words, the mother ordered the girl to pack, and the next morning she put her in the carriage, which headed towards her uncle's house. The girl cried for a long time and regretted her behavior. However, the decision was made and had to accept the punishment.

After a few days, the carriage reached its destination. The girl was greeted by her uncle in town. It was an older man with a long white mustache.

They both marched towards the old house. When they got there, the girl saw a huge mansion surrounded by a huge garden.

When they got inside, my uncle said to his niece:

- Your room is on the first floor. I work a lot, so you will spend most of your time alone. You can enter anywhere except the room on the top floor, the one at the end of the corridor. Swear you'll never go in there!

"I promise you, uncle," replied the child sadly.

Days passed. The girl tried to be polite, despite the fact that she was often alone and could not count on praise. With time, however, after visiting every corner of the old manor, she began to get bored. More and more often she thought about the forbidden room and - whether she wanted it or not - her legs from time to time led her towards it.

One overcast day, she could not stand it anymore and decided to look there. She walked cautiously down the dark corridor towards the secret door. She was tiptoeing, and her breathing was unheard of. When she stood in front of the room, she gently bent down and peered inside through the keyhole. The room was dim, and she saw nothing of the sort. She decided to go in. It was dark inside and very cold. Several old wardrobes stood by the walls, some of the furniture was covered with light canvas. She took a few steps forward. At that moment the door slammed with a bang. The girl ran to them quickly and tried to open them. With no effect. Suddenly she heard a voice behind her back:

- Who you are…? - he was terrible, hoarse. The child was very scared and tried to open the door as soon as possible.

- Who you are? This time she heard the voice clearer, as if the figure was getting closer to her.

The girl started screaming and pounding her fists on the closed door. Then she felt a cold, bony hand on her shoulder. Her heart skipped a beat. Slowly she turned her head to see who was holding her. To her horror, she saw a monstrous, gaunt and wrinkled figure. Her eyes were large, bulging and bloodshot. Broken, yellowed teeth protruded from his twisted mouth.

- Who you are?! The ghost exclaimed, his voice even more hoarse and terrifying.

The girl screamed loudly and pulled the door handle with all her might. This time it worked and the child ran out into the corridor, closing the door behind him. She ran as hard as she could to the ground floor and ran out into the yard. She was relieved to see her uncle returning from work. She threw herself on his neck and, crying, told him what had happened.

This room belonged to my late wife, your aunt, said my uncle. "Nobody's there, but the room has been locked since she died." You shouldn't have gone in there, I forbade you. You're still rude, and that's what you've been punished for for it.

The girl, drowning in tears, apologized to her uncle and promised that she would always be polite.

Since then, she has never disobeyed again. After several months of exemplary behavior, she was allowed to return to her family, where she willingly helped the rest of the household with all the work.

3. Blue city

Far away, next to an oak grove, was the house of elves. They lived in harmony with nature, cultivating wheat and caring for the orchard. All residents were very happy. Only one elf was perpetually dissatisfied. Sikorek was called after him, mainly because he spent the whole days exploring the area, flying on the back of his befriended tit.

Well, fate wanted it so that the local area was hit by a series of tragic storms, during which the entire village was razed to the ground. Some of its small inhabitants died, and the rest fled to all parts of the world. Only Sikorek was away from his place of residence at that time. When, after a few days, he returned from his trip, seeing the enormity of the destruction, he fell to his knees and cried:

"Oh, what a fool I am!" He should be here supporting my brothers. Now I am alone as a finger and will never have a family.

He wiped away his tears and jumped back onto the back of his winged friend.

- Go! The elf shouted. - We'll find a new home. I promise that once we settle down in a place, I won't leave it for a day.

After these words, they flew into the air and headed west. Sikorek has never been to those regions and hoped that maybe he would find a new life there.

They flew for a long time, and the days passed. They finally reached a beautiful kingdom. Its inhabitants dressed only in blue robes, and the buildings were built of blue stones. The brave gnome was small in size compared to any man who passed him, which, however, did not completely discourage him. He decided to live in this strange city. Together with the tit, they built a small nest on a large tree with turquoise leaves, standing in the middle of a picturesque square.

As soon as they settled, Sikorek looked around for a job. A difficult task, however, faced him, as in the world of the "giants" he was not fit for any occupation. He was too small to herd cows, his arms were too short to bake bread, and he was not strong enough to deliver milk to the inhabitants. Resigned after several weeks of unsuccessful searching, he sat down on a small rock and cried aloud. His cry was heard by the daughter of the florist's owner passing by.

- What's the matter, little one? She asked in a sweet voice.

- Ah, beautiful girl. For a long time, fate has not spared me. My home was destroyed by storms, my friends died, and when I finally found a place for myself, I couldn't even afford a hot meal.

The girl took pity on the house elf and led him to her father. He immediately offered him a job. The short stature has proved to be a unique asset in the fight against weeds.

Every morning, Sikorek would dig out of his nest and set off towards the florist's garden. The work was not difficult, but very time-consuming, so he always returned after dark. Happily his days passed. His heart began to beat harder to the florist's daughter, but he knew that she would not want the house elf to be her husband. Thoughts of a beautiful girl began to turn into an obsession. Every evening, after finishing work, the elf would sit for hours by the window of her room and watch his beloved's every move. At first the girl did not mind, but when Sikorek became more and more obtrusive, she anxiously said to her father:

- Father, dear. We have to get rid of this terrible house elf. He follows me, scares off admirers and he has threatened me. He said that if I didn't become his wife, he would cut my finger off at night.

The florist was afraid that something bad could happen to his daughter. However, he was afraid to throw out the house elf, because - as it was believed - they are vengeful creatures with which it is better not to mess with. However, he had no choice but to banish him from the city.

To the dismay of his former employer, Sikorek got furiously furious and swore revenge.

Years have passed since then, and none of the inhabitants of the blue city have seen the house elf. It was during this time that the beautiful daughter of a florist met a candidate for a husband. Still, she was nervous that jealous Sikorek would return and take revenge on them all. The night before the wedding was planned, she could not sleep. It was very quiet in the town, there was no living soul in the street. The girl was lying quietly in her bed when suddenly in the distance she heard a whispering voice.

- You didn't want to be mine, even though I gave you my heart.

The florist's daughter's eyes widened. She ran to the window, but saw no one. She went back to bed and covered herself with the covers up to her head.

"You didn't want to be mine, even though I gave you my heart ..." she heard again, this time the voice was closer.
"... and now someone else is holding your hands," the person who was saying these words seemed to be standing at the door of her house.

- You didn't want to know me, you chased me out, you cursed - someone slowly started climbing to the first floor up the creaking stairs. For a moment no one said anything, but for sure some figure was approaching the girl's room.

Already at the door, her tormentor spoke up.

"You didn't want to be mine, even though I gave you my heart!" And now someone else is holding your hands! It wasn't a whisper this time. The mysterious figure almost screamed furiously. "You didn't want to know me, you chased me, you cursed me!"

The handle slowly turned and the door opened with a groan. The girl hid deeper and closed her eyes. She heard someone take a few steps towards her.

***

When the florist entered the future bride's room in the morning, he did not find his daughter. Nobody knew what happened that night or where the girl was. To this day, there is no trace of it.

4. Ceiling monster

Once upon a time, two sisters lived in a small house on the edge of the forest. They lived with their father.

The girls, despite their young age, were very brave and often went on trips to the forest. Every day they ventured farther and farther from home. Until they got so far that they couldn't come back before dusk.

"We can't go any further in the dark," said the older sister. - We have to stay somewhere, we will go back in the morning.

They did so. They found refuge under one of the larger trees, hugged each other and waited for dark. As night fell, the little sister saw a light in the distance.

"Maybe it's a house," she said. "Let's go over there and ask for a shelter." It's better than sleeping on the ground.

As she said, they did so. The cabin was not far away and they arrived quickly.

They knocked on the door and an old hunter opened it. "What are you doing this far from home, little girls?" He asked in a pleasant voice.

"We got lost in the woods," the older sister began. - Can we spend the night here? We will set off on our way back in the morning. The old hunter agreed and invited the children inside. He offered them bread and soup.

- I rarely have visitors here. But I host these little people for the first time. I must warn you. This is not an ordinary cottage. A terrible monster once lived here with his family. Several children set fire to the place to get rid of the scarecrows. This was only partially successful, as the wraiths hid in the ceiling. I advise you not to approach it, because when you do, they will stick their disgusting hands from the ceiling, drag you inside and devour you.

When the hunter finished his story, he put out the candle and left the room, leaving the girls alone.

The children did not care much about this story, believing he only wanted to scare them. They were not very tired yet and decided to have some fun before going to sleep. The younger sister was a very lively child, she began jumping around the bed with enthusiasm. She jumped higher and higher. After all, it was so high that she could touch the ceiling with her hands. Then great hairy paws emerged from the ceiling. The fingers were tipped with powerful claws. When the girl was close, they grabbed her and pulled her inside. The little girl screamed and defended herself against the tight hug, but it didn't do much. After a while, only her legs were visible.

The older sister, seeing all this, began to scream in terror. She climbed onto the bed and tried to jump high enough to grab her little sister. However, she did not have time, because the terrible monster absorbed her completely. Then a worried hunter burst into the room. He grabbed the larger girl and ran with her outside.

"My sister stayed there," the girl cried.

Unfortunately, we can't do anything about it. The monsters have eaten her, 'the hunter announced sadly. - Come on, baby. I will walk you home.

They walked together through the dark forest. The girl was no longer afraid of the dark. But every now and then she heard shuffling behind her, as if the monsters were following them.

So they quickened their pace. The child was very happy to see his father, who took his daughter in his arms with relief. The family thanked the hunter for his help and he returned to himself.

The girl herself was no longer walking away from home. However, when she passed the place where the hunter's hut stood a few years later, she noticed with horror that there was nothing there, and probably never had been.

5.The cat and the owl

Many years ago, in a distant country, there lived a kitten without a single paw. He was very calm and friendly. He lived on a small farm, far from the city. However, his life was not easy. The hostess thought that it was not suitable for hunting mice, so it is not useful at all. - Who saw it - she kept repeating - so that the cat had to be fed and he brought nothing in return. Time to get rid of this parasite!

The husband of the hostess defended the kitten. He believed that he brought a lot of warmth to their home and was the perfect companion for him. Every evening, when the host was sitting in a large armchair and reading a book, the kitten would jump on his lap and accompany him until the candle went out. However, the good lord could not resist his wife endlessly. One chilly morning he took the kitten and, as the landlady wished, went with it to the river.

"I'm sorry, my little friend," he said goodbye. - This is the will of my wife.

After a while, he put the toddler in the bag and threw it into the water. He couldn't watch the kitten sink, so he quickly turned and walked towards the farm.

Meanwhile, the smart animal managed to free itself. The water carried him away from home. Coming ashore, he realized that he was in an unknown place.

"Too bad," he said sadly. - I have nothing to go back to the farm. I have to learn to hunt so as not to starve to death.

The kitten without a paw lives in a great forest. Every day he tried to hunt a small animal, but his prey was mostly beetles and other small creatures. He finally started to like the new house. He also met an old owl, which was never farther than near her tree, so she eagerly asked him about life on the farm.

“And these piglets,” she said, “are they good to eat?”

- Good good! - boasted the cat, as if he himself made sure that the pork was available at home.

- And these chickens? Good?

- The best meat in the world! The hostess made delicious soup out of them.

- And chicken eggs? Good?

- I personally chose the best ones in the henhouse!

The owl stared at the cat in disbelief. How could such a toddler, without a single hand, do it all by himself? However, the stories of her young friend captured the owl’s imagination. She wanted to know the world around them. Since she was already old, she asked the cat to travel with her. She would need the help of such a great hunter.

The next day, they set off together in an unknown direction. They wandered for days, and the owl could not get a glimpse of the beautiful views that unfolded around them. On the way, they ate worms and berries. One day they passed a farm. Happy piglets were splashing in the mud right next to the farm.

- Look! The owl shouted to her companion. - Exactly as you described to me! I’m fed up with worms! I wish you could hunt one of them for dinner tonight.

The cat was very worried, but decided to undertake this task. It lurked and lurked. He walked around the herd of pigs. It took a long time, and the owl was getting impatient. Finally, the little hunter lunged at the little piglet with all his might. He clawed his claws to his back and jabbed his fangs into his flesh. The pig looked quite surprised. After a while she laughed derisively and threw the kitten into the mud. As she walked away, she crushed him with her hoof.

The owl stared in disbelief at this comic situation. She decided that the piglets on her friend’s farm must have been much smaller. They went on. As they passed the henhouse, the bird said again:

If not pork, bring us eggs. I promise this is my last request. We will hide in the bushes, eat eggs and rest.

The cat agreed to it. After all, stealing eggs can’t be very difficult. He started at the entrance and stepped cautiously inside. The owl lost sight of him. Nothing happened for a long moment. Suddenly there was a loud meow. A frightened cat ran out of the henhouse, followed by three angry chickens. The animal had one egg in its teeth and escaped as fast as it could in its paws. He reached the owl and together they disappeared into the bushes. Once they were safe, the owl wanted to inspect the prey. But the kitten did it for the first time and squeezed the egg too hard with his teeth. All the contents drained out in the escape from the hens. At that moment, the owl understood that the cat had deceived her. He was not a hunter, he did not hunt large animals, and he did not collect eggs from a henhouse. She was furious and hungry.

- Well, what am I going to eat for dinner now ...? She was talking towards the cat, simultaneously twisting her head to the side, as owls are used to. She caught up with the cat in one leap, sticking her claws into it. After a while, she was full and continued her journey herself.

6. Island

Once upon a time there was a great lake. It was so huge that no one has ever managed to walk around it or swim across it. In its center was a small island that few people knew about.

There was a town on the very shore with only 20 inhabitants. A young couple lived there and they tried very hard to have a child, but to no avail. Eventually, my wife broke down completely. She stopped getting out of bed and stared absentmindedly through the window all day. My husband was worried about his beloved and wanted to help her as soon as possible. One day he confided his problems to an old fisherman.

- Young man - said the elderly gentleman, - I think I can advise you. Well, I heard that there is a small island in the middle of the lake. A witch who knows all spells lives on it. She could help you. Be careful though, there have been many daredevils trying to find the island. To this day, no one has managed to return.

Without thinking, the husband set off on a dangerous journey. He had been sailing for a very long time, and for many days he could not see land on the horizon. As his fate grew uncertain, he saw a small island in the distance. He was overjoyed and swam as close as possible.
Unfortunately, he was not able to land on the shore, he saw a huge ten-meter cliff. He sailed around the island, but everywhere the shore was high. Ultimately, he decided to climb the rocks. He dropped the anchor and jumped into the water, and after a while he swam to the cliff. The climbing was extremely easy for him and after a few minutes he was standing on level ground.

There were only a few trees on the island, a farm with sheep and a small hut with chickens running around happily. The young man courageously moved on. He knocked on the door.

- Who the hell did they get? An old woman's voice came from behind the door.

- My name is Theodore. I come from the village from the lake shore.

- What do you want from me? I wasn't inviting anyone!

- I just want to ask you for help. We cannot have children with my wife. If you help us, I will pay you handsomely for this service.

There was silence for a moment. Suddenly the door opened and the old woman stepped out into the yard. She might even be over a hundred years old.

"I'll help you," she said to the young man with a mocking smile, "but I don't want any money for it." I'll give you a potion. If your wife drinks it at midnight, there will be three children in your life at regular intervals.

- It's wonderful! Theodore exclaimed happily. -What do you want in return, good woman?

- One of the children will be a girl. As soon as she is born, you will bring her to me. Such a treat will be the best reward for me.

The man was very scared of such an agreement, but, seeing it as the only chance for an offspring, agreed.

Upon his return, he told his wife everything. The woman was so happy that on the first night she drank the mysterious mixture. In the same year, their first son was born. Over the next few years, another healthy boy appeared in their lives.

When the spouses were expecting another child, they became anxious. The wife cried all night.

"We won't take our daughter to her," her husband said finally. - What will the stupid old woman do to us. Not even a boat! Anyway, years have passed, probably already biting the sand, a mean witch.

A few months later, a beautiful baby was born. Parents named her Lilia.

The girl was developing very well. When she turned 16, she was considered the most beautiful maiden in the entire kingdom. Her parents had long forgotten the oath they had taken. Unfortunately, the witch did not forget. Angry every day, she devised revenge.

- They don't want to bring me one child like they promised! So they will lose all of them, the old woman laughed in her hut.

Lilia could not sleep for a long time that same night. Suddenly she heard a voice coming from the coast.

- Help! Help!

The girl, without thinking much, quickly dressed and ran out into the yard. Her older brother stood in the way:

- It's dangerous. I'll help that person, and you go back to your room.

Lilia obediently returned home. The next day she was awakened by her mother's lamentation. One of the fishermen saw her older son get into the water and walk until he disappeared under the surface of the lake.

The family could not recover from this loss for a long time. Unfortunately, the situation repeated itself after some time. This time, the middle brother followed suit, and he, too, never came home again.

In despair, parents understood who was summoning their children. They decided to leave the village far into the kingdom to protect their youngest daughter.

They thought they had managed to trick the witch, because they lived many years peacefully in their new home. The witch, however, followed them and knew exactly where they lived. One day, when the parents went out to harvest the crops, their daughter was left alone. The witch, taking advantage of this moment, stormed into their home. The terrified girl hid in the wardrobe. But it was to no avail. The old woman opened the door and pulled Lilia by the hair. She pulled on her until she ripped all her hair out and disfigured her beautiful face.

"I will let you survive," said the smug witch, "let your face remind your parents of a broken oath for the rest of your life!" - saying this, she disappeared, never to return.

7. The windmill thief

A long time ago, there was a little girl in a small town. She lived with her parents in a modest house.

My father worked in a nearby sawmill, and my mother worked in folk art. Every day the woman went to the back of the house to devote herself completely to her passion. She made wooden figurines, garden gnomes, angels and small animals. Each time she was accompanied by her daughter, who closely followed her mother's work.

One day, while the little girl was cleaning the house eagerly, her mother came up to her.

"Dear child," she said, "you are helping me so bravely." We don't have much fortune, and I know you'd like more toys. I did something special for you.

The woman left for a moment, then returned with a small, colorful pinwheel. The girl was very happy and as soon as she finished cleaning, she took her new toy and ran out to play in the clearing.

She danced in all directions, swinging the fan. It swirled beautifully in the wind and shimmered with many colors. The whole fun was watched by a stranger. He approached the child and said:

- What are you having so much fun, little girl?

"My parents won't let me talk to strangers," said the girl, and began walking quickly towards the house.

The stranger, who had never seen a fan like this before, followed her.

- Where did you get such a miracle? He continued. The girl was silent.

She quickened her pace, the house was already visible from afar.

- You'd better tell me, I'd like to have one too.

The stranger was walking next to her, which made her heart dread.

She started to run, but it was to no avail as the man started to run after her. The little one was quite fast, so it was hard to catch up with her. The Lord, however, had long legs and quickly caught up with his victim. He grabbed the girl by the shoulders and started screaming that she would give him a colorful miracle. Fortunately, they were close to the house and their mother saw them through the window. She ran out into the yard. The stranger, as soon as he noticed her, snatched the pinwheel from the girl's hand and began to run away. After a while, there was no trace of him. The girl snuggled into her mother's arms and cried out.

Moments later, my father returned from work. His wife quickly told him what had happened. This made him very angry. He went into town and asked every passerby if he had seen the thief. Unfortunately for him, no one saw the stranger. Soon the rest of the family joined the search, and then the whole town.

Meanwhile, the thief took advantage of the inattention of the inhabitants and robbed every house in the city in turn. Nobody knew where the stranger was and where he stored all the stolen things. The sheriff issued an arrest warrant offering ten gold coins for each useful piece of information. Nobody managed to find the thief, until one day a brave lumberjack came to the town. He traveled the entire kingdom in search of employment. He had a hard time finding anything, so he figured he would look for a thief to get his reward and patch up his budget a little.

The woodcutter began his search by visiting a nearby forest. As he penetrated every corner of it, he encountered a lonely owl. This surprised him greatly, because the bird, instead of sitting in a tree, like the rest of the species, walked happily along the forest path.

- Where are you going, owl? Asked the lumberjack amused.

- I'm an old owl. However, I am still trying to enjoy life and that is why I visit the whole kingdom.

"Tell me, old woman, haven't you seen a stranger here by any chance who would be carrying various objects?"

"Yes," she said, "he has passed me several times." Each time it carried something different. If you go this way, you will surely find it.

The woodcutter thanked for help and moved on. In fact, after a few hours of wandering, he saw a small hut. It stood completely aloof, and had it not been for the help of the owl, he would never have found it. He looked inside, and there the thief lay comfortably on the pile of stolen things, carelessly playing with the fan. The woodcutter took his ax in his hand and struck with all his might on the wooden door of the cottage. The stranger was so scared that he fell with a crash to the floor.

- I got you! The lumberjack shouted.

He grabbed the thief by the shirt and with an efficient movement he bound his legs and arms. Then he loaded all the things on a wheelbarrow standing by the hut, and threw the thug himself upstairs. So loaded, he dragged it on the road with great effort. However, he did not notice that in the meantime the thief had slipped down, fell down the path and hid in the bushes.

After a long journey, the lumberjack reached the town. Unfortunately for him, he did not know anyone there and the residents decided that he was the mysterious thief who, fearing punishment, decided to return all the stolen items. Even the girl's assurances that it was not this person who stole her pinwheel did not help. Who would believe a little child? The girl's mother could not describe the perpetrator and decided herself that it was the lumberjack who had robbed the town.

Thus, instead of ten gold coins, the brave lumberjack was punished with several months of arrest. He also had to return all his gold coins as compensation.

8.Baba Yaga and the Witch

Away from the big city, but also from smaller villages, there were two houses. Each of them looked glum.

One wooden hut had a collapsed roof, completely covered with straw. In the garden, the flowers withered and weeds developed. The whole thing was surrounded by a gray fence, with some boards missing here and there. Baba Yaga lived in the hut.

The second cabin, all brick, was covered with ivy. There weren't even any dead flowers in the garden, but in the middle you could see a small puddle in which a duck was trying to swim. The witch lived there.

Both old men, despite their close proximity, harbored a real hatred for each other. Every day, everyone was trying to trick her rival. And so once the Witch found a lot of dead mice in her pond, another time Baba Yaga noticed that the straw from her roof had been torn off. Their dispute lasted for years and there was no way of reconciliation in sight.

It was so fate that one day a beautiful prince passed by on a white horse. He separated from his group during the hunt and could not find a way back to the kingdom. When he saw two huts, he decided to ask for directions. He dismounted in front of the brick house, went to the door and called:

- Hi! Is anybody out there? I wanted to ask which way should I go to the castle.

The witch opened the curtain and looked at the uninvited guest through the window. She was not in the habit of receiving passers-by, but this young man charmed her completely.

"Please, come in," the old woman said, opening the door ajar. - Sit down, you must be tired. You're lucky, I was just sitting at the table to eat frog eye soup. Please join me.

The prince winced at the sight of the green and white slush. However, he did not want to offend the hostess, so he thanked him and sat down at the table. It was hard for him to swallow the disgusting dish, but he did so, hoping to win the Witch's sympathy and guide him home.

- Tell me, boy, where did you come from in this remote area? She licked her lips as she said it.

- I was on a hunt and I chased a beautiful deer. I followed him for a long time, but I was not able to hunt him down. After a while, I realized that I couldn't find my companions. Fortunately, I found this house, madam.

The witch clapped with delight. The Prince referred to her as a lady, which was not very common for her. It wasn't really happening to her at all.

"According to your clothes, my lord, you are the son of a king."

- That's right.

"So the lady you marry, my lord, will become queen in the future," the woman continued.

- Yes, in the future, yes. Why are you asking, madam?

The witch ran towards him. Her eyes shone with delight.

- It is no accident, my dear, that you are here. Take me to the castle. I will serve you faithfully as your wife!

The prince almost overturned his chair with an impression. Only now did he realize who welcomed him. The decoration of the room was mainly the skulls of small animals, there was a stench of blood and general decay everywhere. He realized that if he did not agree to the Witch's request, he could face severe punishment.

When he was about to agree to her proposal, Baba Yaga burst into the house and watched the whole event through the window.

"Hurry, boy," she screamed, "let's run, this is the evil Witch."

The prince, without thinking much, ran after the old woman to her wooden house. The witch was left alone. Unfortunately, she could not run after the fugitive, because her cunning neighbor used a spell that meant that no one behind her and those invited by her could cross the threshold of her house.

Meanwhile, in the house next door, a young man thanked the old woman for saving her.

- How can I repay you, dear woman?

Oh boy! I'm glad you asked. Before you leave, I would like to ask you to bring me sacks of potatoes from the cellar. I am very old and it is too much effort for me.

- Of course! No problem! The overjoyed prince approached the door from the basement with his deliverer. He went in first and started looking for the bag. He couldn't find anything like that. The room was completely empty. Only a table with a lit candle stood in the center, and a chair next to it.

- Good woman, there's nothing here! He shouted. In response, all he heard was the sound of the door closing and the latch closed. Terrified, he ran to the exit and started screaming for her to let him go.

"I am not as stupid as my neighbor," Baba Yaga said proudly. - I also want to be your wife and sit on the throne! I realize that if we got to the castle together now, you would have quickly thrown me into the dungeon, and the next day you would have sentenced me to the gallows. Oh no. I'll make a special broth. Thanks to him, you will feel a real, eternal feeling for me. Be patient my dear, it won't take long. Saying so, she went to the kitchen, where a broth was already boiling in a large cauldron.

The prince broke down completely. He knew there was no chance of salvation anymore. He sat down at the table and wept bitterly. His lament was heard by a duck that was swimming in a puddle in the Witch's yard. She tracked to the only small window in the basement and called for the prince.

- I can help you. Kwa! - She said, sticking her beak inside.

- Oh no! Cried the young man getting up from the chair.

- I know who you are! It was that witch who sent you, I won't be fooled!

- Kwa! I am a prisoner. and so do you. A long time ago, this old woman cast a spell on me because she was jealous of my beauty. The charm will only be lifted when I go far enough from her home. Kwa! I never did it myself, because she always caught me, but you have a good chance.

The prince knew he had no choice but to trust the ugly duck.

- Okay. What should I do?

- Kwa! When Baba Yaga brings you the brew, take it and pour it over the candle. The flame will become very bright and it will blind the old woman for a while. You will then have a moment to run out and mount your horse. Kwa! I will wait with your horse.

The young man did as instructed by the duck. As soon as the whole room was illuminated by intense light, Baba Yaga screamed, covering her eyes. At this point, the prince ran out of the basement, closing the door behind him and locking the bolt.

He ran quickly outside and mounted his horse. As he was about to leave, he heard a voice behind him.

- You don't want to leave me here, do you? Kwa! We had a deal.

The prince did not want to take the duck and hesitated for a moment.

- Know one thing, - said the bird,

- I know which way to go, and you don't.

The prince saw this as a sufficient argument. He picked up the duck, put it in the bag and slung it over his shoulder, and together they rushed to the castle.

They galloped for a long time, and the farther they were from the huts of two old women, the heavier the bag on the prince's shoulder became. In the end, the boy could not bear the weight and stopped the horse. When he looked in the bag, he was terribly amazed. Instead of a duck, a girl of extraordinary beauty appeared to him. He fell in love with her at first sight. They reached the castle as fiancés.

9. Cosmic tree

There was a small hut in the middle of a great gravel desert. It was inhabited by a certain scholar who had long ago worked for the king himself. However, he was banished from the kingdom because he questioned the theories of the local priest. The scholar, hailed as a heretic, had to leave his home. Seeking peace, he found a place where a human foot has never stopped. Here he could conduct research and make various experiments, knowing that no one would disturb him.

One night, while the scientist was observing the sky as usual, taking notes, something unusual happened. Suddenly, one of the stars started racing across the sky. He seemed to be getting closer to the scientist. Finally, the mysterious object hit the ground with a great bang, a few meters from the hut. The sage slowly approached the small indentation that the star had left behind. Seeing that there was nothing there, he was very surprised. He was so tired that he decided to go to sleep and come back to the matter first thing in the morning.

As soon as the sun broke over the horizon, the scientist ran to the place of impact. What he saw there made him dread. Now, instead of a small recess, there was a huge tree in front of him. Its bark and branches were completely black. It looked dead because it had no leaves. The trunk was so thick that it was impossible to hold your arms around it.

The scientist began to study a strange plant, but it was no different from any other tree on earth. He could have sworn, however, that she came from the stars and that her arrival was not a coincidence. Every six months the man was visited by his old friend, a blacksmith from the royal court. It also so happened that the blacksmith's visit happened just a few days after the mysterious tree had grown.

- And what has grown up here, dear friend? The smith said, dismounting from his horse.

- My dear, a strange thing has happened. One night a seed came to me from the stars. The tree grew to this size in just one day.

- It's amazing! The blacksmith walked around the tree with admiration.

- Do you water them sometimes? It looks like it's completely withered away.

- I water them sometimes, but I don't see that it affects them.

Both friends went to the hut for dinner. They talked with each other for a long time about what was going on outside. About the fact that the king is short of money and is in danger of bankruptcy. The people of the kingdom are becoming increasingly dissatisfied and are threatening to rise.

"So, my dear friend," continued the smith, "who knows, maybe a day will come when I will have to move to you." You know when it gets very bad there.

"Know that you are always welcome here," said the scholar, escorting his friend to the door. As they said goodbye, a light blinded them. They both looked at the tree and couldn't believe their eyes. A golden walnut hung from one of the branches. The men ran up to him and looked at him.

- What's this? Asked the blacksmith.

"It looks like pure gold," the scientist broke the walnut with one movement of his hand, then handed it to his friend. - Please take this. In these times, it will be more useful to you than to me.

The blacksmith thanked him with all his heart and started back.

The news that there is a tree in the desert that bears golden nuts spread very quickly throughout the kingdom. But no one except the blacksmith knew how to get to him. Rumors of a space tree also reached the king himself, who ordered a scientist friend to be brought.

"Hello, dear man," the king thundered to his guest. "I hear that you have information that gives our kingdom a chance to recover from its financial downturn.

The blacksmith was very confused. He did not want to reveal his friend's secret, but the king gave him no choice. If he does not indicate where the tree grows, he will be thrown into the dungeon forever. Like it or not, he led the king's envoys into the desert. The scholar had not expected a visit from anyone, and was therefore completely devoted to his work. But when he heard the sound of horses approaching, he leaned out of the hut. Three people dragged him out of the house and several others started digging holes around the black tree.

- Stop! - shouted the scientist - we do not know what this plant is, we do not know what it is capable of.

Then black clouds began to arrive from all sides, and after a while the sky was already very dark. The wind was blowing at dizzying speed and the first raindrops appeared. Suddenly the scientist heard a scream. He could not see what was happening to the invaders, because visibility was getting worse. There were screams everywhere, every now and then you could see the roots of a black tree flying around. Blood stains covered the ground. The scientist began to run forward. He ran into a certain person who was also on the run. It was a blacksmith. The friends hugged with relief and together they moved as fast as possible, as far as possible from the tree. They hid behind a large rock and tried to wait out the whole situation. When the screams had died down completely and the clouds seemed to thin out, they came out of hiding.

The tree was still standing in the same place. Untouched. The king's envoys were nowhere to be found. Only the traces of a fight on the gravel revealed what had just happened there.

- What could have happened? The smith asked.

"I don't know," the scientist mused. - Looks like the tree was resisting relocation. Apparently he feels good here.

Both friends went to the hut. The blacksmith decided not to go back to the kingdom anymore and live with his friend, and since no one else knew how to get to this place, no one came over them anymore.

10. Scary Old Man

Long ago, it was believed that naughty children were taken by the Scary Grandpa. He looks for children who do not clean the house, do not listen to their parents or make an ugly speech. As soon as such a child is left alone, he quickly grabs him and takes him away forever. A father and his daughter lived in a town. He had moved there recently, right after the loss of his younger daughter, who disappeared under mysterious circumstances. They both lived peacefully and happily. Father spoiled his only child and eventually she began to behave inappropriately. She didn't say "hello" or "thank you" to neighbors when she got something. She did not clean the room and often did not come home overnight.

"You'll see," my father used to say. - If you don't stop misbehaving, Dziad will come and take you!

- Huh! The girl mocked. - These are fairy tales good for small children. I am the greatest and I am entitled to everything. I'm not going to apologize for that.

And it was like that every day.

Once a father asked his daughter to go get hen eggs. The girl agreed, took the money and went to the market. There were many great items there, including a fabulously colored ball.

- I must have her! She shouted with delight.

Unfortunately, if she had bought a toy, it would not have been enough for eggs.

- I already know! I'll buy a ball and put it under my dress. And I will tell my father that my money has been stolen.

So she did. The father was worried about the loss of money, but was glad the thief had done nothing wrong to his child.

The next day he sent his daughter back to the market for chicken eggs. This time the girl caught the eye of a beautiful pink hair ribbon.

If it worked once, she thought, it will also work this time.

The child bought the ribbon and put it in his pocket. Upon returning home, the girl announced that the money had fallen into the river as she bent over it to wash her hands.

The man was very worried that he had lost more money, but also this time he was glad that at least the girl had not fallen into the river. The next day the father handed the girl the last of his money, saying:

- This is our last money, we won't have any more by the end of the month. Please buy as many hens as possible, and maybe we'll make it until the next payday.

The girl took the money and ran to the market. This time, she decided to buy only eggs. However, when she passed the hat stand, one of them delighted her especially.

- I'll buy something for the last time. After all, I came to the market so many times for shopping that I deserved it.

This time the girl found no excuse for the lack of money. The angry father ordered his daughter to take all items purchased without permission and sell them to get the money back. The child reluctantly picked up a hat, ribbon, and ball and headed for the market. After she sold her belongings, she returned home with a sack full of gold coins.

"I'm glad you got your money back," my father said sternly. - However, you will not miss the punishment. Go to your room.

- No! The girl shouted and left the house, slamming the door.

She walked for a long time through the whole city, which was getting emptier and emptier by the hour. After all, there was no one in the streets. The child was walking along the narrow street when suddenly, facing him, he saw a gloomy figure.

I have been watching you for a long time - said the bogeyman, slowly approaching the girl. It was the Scary Old Man that the adults had warned her about. The little girl started to run away, but Dziad caught up with her without much problem. He reached out, grabbed her, and pressed her tightly against him so that she couldn't move. They both disappeared into the dark.

The girl lost consciousness.

When she woke up, she couldn't recognize where she was. It was like a cave, but furnished like an ordinary house. To her right were large cages in which human skeletons lay limply. She, too, was in one of these cages, but standing in the center of the room. Suddenly, the Scary Old Man emerged from the darkness.

"Welcome to my humble cottage," he said hoarsely. - This is where all naughty kids end up. As you can imagine, they stay here forever!

The girl started crying. The Scary Old Man moved her cage to the others and walked away into the shadows. She was left alone.

- Psst! - She heard a voice coming from a nearby cage. - Hi!

- Who's there? The girl asked in horror.

"My name is Jurek," the boy's round face emerged from the darkness.

- Are you new?

- I think so…

- Cool! Jurek rejoiced. - There was no one here for a long time. Don't worry, nothing will happen to us. Contrary to what they say, the Scary Grandpa does not eat children.

- Then why are there skeletons in these cages? The girl asked.

The boy fell silent. He lowered his head and said softly, "He's leaving us here ... in these cages, forever."

The girl was terrified. She cried even more. She wished she had listened to her father and that she had left the house without permission.

Over time, the children became friends with each other. The Scary Old Man appeared rarely. He disappeared for days and no one knew where he was since he was not in his own house. The girl could not come to terms with the thought that she was supposed to stay here for the rest of her life and she would never see her father again.

"Jurek," she said one day, "we have to get out of here."

- Heh, you can't escape from here.

- Look at me - the little girl revealed her belly - he does not feed us and I am already very thin. I'll try to squeeze through the bars.

The girl put her head through the bars and then gently put the rest of her body so that after a while she was free. She ran to Jurek's cage and helped him through. The children, holding hands, ran out of the cave. They wandered through a very dense forest that separated the cave from the ordinary world.

When Grandfather returned to his home and noticed that the children were gone, he howled terribly. The wind blew the sound of a scream all over the forest, chilling the little fugitives' blood in the veins. The bogeyman was unable to find the children in the dense forest and, after a few days of searching, gave up.

Meanwhile, Jurek and the girl were wandering in the forest.

"I'm sorry," the boy worried. - I don't know how we can get out of this boron.

After a few days, a large tree with a door and two windows stood in their way. The girl knocked inside.

- Who's there? - heard a nice female voice from behind the door.

- My name is Zuzia. The Scary Old Man trapped us. We ran away and now we can't get home.

A woman quickly emerged from the strange cottage. It turned out that she once had three sons. They were real rascals. They pranked all the time and never listened to their mother. One day, all three were taken by the Scary Grandfather, and the woman, in search of her sons, reached this forest. However, she never managed to find them.

"Follow me," she said to the refugees, "I will take you to the city."

After a long journey, Zuzia happily hugged her father. Jurek was not that lucky. It turned out that after the boy's disappearance, his family moved in an unknown direction and they were not heard of. The woman felt sorry.

- I lost my sons and you lost your family. Come home with me and I will be your mother forever.

So the boy went to the forest with his new mother and found true happiness.

Jurek and Zuzia lived happily ever after. The Scary Dziad, however, was always watching them closely.

11. The Great River

Legend has it that there was a river on which even the bravest fishermen were afraid to swim. It was so wide that it was difficult to see the other side. The people of the village competed in tales of a mysterious creature that kidnapped boats and anyone who only got even one foot into the water.

The kingdom in which the town was located was very poor. The king's treasury had been empty for a long time and all his subjects had a hard time. And while rumors have been heard that a tree that bears golden nuts has been found, no one has confirmed it.

The Forbidden River ran through three neighboring kingdoms. Therefore, a great reward has been set for the capture of the hijacker. The poor king saw it as an opportunity to improve his and his subjects' well-being. He summoned all the fishermen in the kingdom and said:

- I invited you here because I have an unusual request for you. You must have heard that our two neighbors jointly presented a prize for capturing those who drown the boats on the Great River. I promise that whoever brings me the head of the offender will receive one percent of this reward from me.

The fishermen were very happy. The sum was considerable and each of them immediately started preparing the expedition. Only one fisherman remained in the hall, alone with the king. He was the oldest inhabitant of the city from the river.

- Do you have any more questions, old man? The king asked.

"Yes, my lord," replied the fisherman, bowing. - Who are we hunting? Are these pirates? Or is the legend of the monster true?

"I cannot answer your questions, good man," replied the ruler solemnly. - It will certainly not be an easy journey and many men may perish.

The old man nodded and went home. He lived in a small brick house right on the Great River. As soon as he got there, his wife met him. The old woman listened anxiously to what her husband heard in the castle.

"You shouldn't go," she said finally. - Let the young people take care of it.

- Our home and land will be taken from us soon. We still have many years of life ahead of us and I would rather live in a warm house to the end than somewhere in the street. What else is left for me? Don't worry about me, my dear. "That said, he went to prepare his boat."

The fisherman got up at dawn, said goodbye to his wife and went out into deep water. Once he was in the middle of the river so that he could see both banks, he stopped rowing and let the boat go with the current. He hadn't seen anything out of the ordinary all day. Only a few fishermen passed him, mocking him at his old age.

- Come home, Grandpa! They shouted.

The old man did not care about gibes and continued to do his job. As night fell and the moon brightened up the area, the old fisherman fell asleep. The sudden rocking of the boat woke him. As if something huge swam right by. The fisherman saw the outline of an extremely large animal just below the surface of the water. It was aimed at a boat that was nearby. Its owners dropped the anchor and slept well. The mysterious shape stopped under the boat, suddenly large tentacles wrapped around her on all sides. The fishermen didn't stand a chance. The boat was pulled under the water with them so quickly that people did not even have time to scream.

Watching all this, the old fisherman was speechless. The creature began swimming towards him.

- What should I do? He said to himself.

As soon as the first tentacle emerged from the water, the old man quickly struck it with his oar, so that it quickly returned to the water. The creature seemed surprised that anyone could oppose it. After a while, he completely emerged from the water to look at the daredevil who dared to hit him. The creature was huge and had huge eyes.

- Who are you? Sounded the monster.

- I'm an old fisherman. I have come to put an end to your rule on the Great River.

Hearing this, the creature laughed with such force that waves rose in the river.

- How do you want to do this?

The old man had no idea. He remembered, however, that his wife had given him a strong poison before she left. The good woman thought she could somehow be served to the creature to eat. The fisherman took out a bottle of decoction.

- What have you got there, old man?

- This? The fisherman looked surprised. - That's what I'll beat you with. This is a special brew for extraordinary strength. If I drink it, I'll be bigger than you and easily defeat you!

- Give it back to me! - the monster snatched the poison from the old man and drank it quickly. - And who is wiser, old man?

- I! The fisherman replied calmly.

At that moment, the creature rolled its eyes inward, exhaled its last breath, and fell lifeless. The dead monster floated freely in the water. The old man grabbed one of the tentacles and tied it with a rope to the boat.

The way back was very difficult. It was hard for an aged fisherman to row with such luggage up the river. His return took weeks and his wife had given up hope that he would come home safe and sound.

But when he finally came back, she was very happy.

"Run to inform the king," the fisherman ordered.

On the same day, the king handed over the monster's head to his neighbors, and he rewarded the elderly couple handsomely, which allowed them to live peacefully for many more years.

12. Queen of spirits

Formerly the world of the dead was ruled by a good queen. It was said that in life she was a beautiful girl, but she never experienced the taste of true love. Her lover chose another woman, which contributed to the premature death of the queen. And she died because her heart was broken.

Even though she was a great ruler, adored by all souls, she never smiled. She was always surrounded by sadness. She could wander the Earth for hours, observing the happiness of living people.

Ah, she thought, how beautiful it would be to be born again and live your life differently.

However, it was not possible. No one has ever managed to return from the world of the dead.

In the realm of souls, time stood still. Nobody was in a hurry, nobody hurt anyone. Each ghost only seemed to exist because of the memories of a past life. Only the ghosts of people who had been killed by others tended to take revenge on their oppressors. It also happened that when a person was very attached to a given place, his soul was unable to leave him, which usually caused fear in the hearts of new tenants. The souls of the prematurely deceased were bored with the melancholy surrounding the land of the dead. They were entertained by playing all sorts of pranks.

Many virgins who took their own lives through heartbreak later visited their would-be husbands or partners. However, when they entered the world of souls, they kept their distance from their recent tormentors at all costs.

Only the Queen made no attempt to cheer herself up by harassing her still living fiance. She believed that it was clearly not written to her. Her soul calmed down during the nightly trips. She visited villages, looked through windows, watched sleeping people. She never made her presence known and did not hurt anyone.

It so happened that one night her spirit reached a small village at the foot of the old mountains. There was a young man who was not much older than the queen on the last day of her life. He was a man with a good heart and extraordinary beauty. And what does not happen often - the queen, visiting him every night, gradually fell in love with him. Every day she waited only for the sun to hide below the horizon and the first stars to appear in the sky, so that she could go back to that village.

One evening, the Queen watched her lover as usual. He was preparing dinner with his mother. When they were both seated, the boy's mother said:

- Son. You are a beautiful and wise young man, so I am surprised that there is still no virgin in your heart.

- Dear mother. I will not give my heart to any other girl. I am waiting for a special person who will change my life for the better. Patience, dear mother.

Hearing this, the Queen was overjoyed. She felt that it was she who was written to this young man. After a while, however, she became sad because she remembered that she no longer belonged to this world. With her head bowed, she moved away from the window. Slowly she walked down the main road towards the forest. Before she left town, she passed the old woman sitting on the bench in front of her house.

- Who's there? The old woman said.

The Queen, unaccustomed to being noticed by anyone, did not stop and continued walking.

"Don't walk away while I'm talking to you, you naughty girl!" Grandma shouted again, turning her head towards the ghost. This already caught the spirit. She quickly came up to the old woman and asked:

- You see me?

- Of course! I am not blind.

"But I am not… here," the queen began hesitantly.

- Heh - laughed the old woman, getting up from the bench. She headed for the door to the house and opened it - I know you are a ghost, my dear. The women in my family already have such a gift, we see and hear you. "Please come in and tell me what's bothering you."

The Queen followed the old lady. At home, she told her about what her life on earth was like, how her soul could not have peace. At the end, she also told her about the feeling that had recently appeared in her heart.

"I have yet to come across such a story," said my grandmother curiously, "for a ghost to fall in love with a living being." Extremely! But don't worry. I know how to help you. Well, I am able to bring you back to life when you lost it, that is - as I can see - when you were 17 years old.

- Really? Is it possible? The queen could not believe the words of the old woman.

- Of course. But nothing is for free. My time on earth is drawing to a close. I feel like I have a few days left. If, on the day of my death, you hand over the crown of the queen of the afterlife to me, you will come back to life. Do you want to relinquish your throne?

- Oh yes! I'd rather live with him like a peasant than all eternity as a queen but without him. - So be it.

The queen spent the next few days near the old woman. When the day came when the old lady was to end her life, the ruler kept her word and gave her her crown. After a while, she felt the warmth surrounding her. The skin is no longer transparent and the hair is shiny. After a few minutes, she was standing with her bare feet on the path warmed by the sun. She was wearing a light, flowing dress, her hair was waist-length. She took a deep breath and smelled the scent of wildflowers and trees for the first time in years. All in larks, she set off towards her beloved's hut. When she got there, she noticed that the boy was in front of the house. He was preparing firewood. As soon as he saw a beautiful girl, he was speechless.

"Hello," she said with a smile.

- W ... hello, who are you?

I have come from far away to meet you.

The young man fell in love immediately. The girl moved in with him that same day, and they got married shortly thereafter. They lived together for many years and had a large family. The Queen finally felt what happy love was.

13. A fairy tale about a unicorn

A long time ago, in a magical forest, there lived a beautiful unicorn. His coat was so white that it shone in the sun, and the horn rising from his head was shimmering with all the colors of the rainbow. It was the only such creature in the area.

All day long he wandered around the meadow and nibbled magic flowers and mushrooms. His life would be very happy if it weren't for the fact that he felt very lonely. He had no friends or family. He spent all his days alone. After all, he was so upset that he decided to leave the magic forest in search of companionship. His journey took days. His hooves were already sore. Fortunately - before he exhausted himself completely - he reached a small human settlement. There was a school on the sidelines, and that was where he went first. He decided that the children would be perfect companions.

When he got there, he saw a little boy in front of the entrance to the school.

"Hello, little boy," he whined pleasantly.

"Hello," answered the child, without even looking up from the book he was reading.

- I'm a lonely unicorn. Do you want to be my friend?

"No," the boy replied shortly.

- But why not?

- I don't believe in unicorns. They don't exist. With that, the little boy hid in the middle of the school.

The unicorn was left alone and very confused. He didn't understand how anyone could disbelieve him when he was here, real, flesh and blood. Not discouraged by this failure, he continued towards the town. However, he was also not lucky there. The passing people ignored him and didn't even look at him. Every now and then he only heard: "unicorns do not exist", "they are only in fairy tales for children", "there is no such thing in the world".

After a few days of trying, the young unicorn finally gave up and disappeared. Because if you don't believe in unicorns, they cease to exist.

14. The Sorceress

Behind the mountains, beyond the forests, and beyond two small rivers, lived a beautiful girl. She lived completely alone in a small cottage on the side of a hill. She was accompanied only by colorful, beautiful butterflies, who were always eager to help her in everything. However, this was not an ordinary child. She had different powers and a wand that could conjure up anything she dreamed of.

One day, a couple of thieves passed by her house. Pyrlak and Seweryn.

Look, said Pyrlak to Seweryn, what a perfect house. We could live here and store anything we steal here. In this outback, no one would ever find us!

"But I think someone lives here," said Seweryn.

I checked. It's just a little girl. We'll chase her out and take her hut.

Both men were very confident. They went to the door and knocked. The door opened by itself, and from the depths of the cabin all they heard was an invitation to go inside.

- Why did the door open by itself? Seweryn was worried.

The two thieves entered the house and looked around. The little housekeeper was nowhere to be found.

- Who are you? Suddenly they heard a child's voice. However, they could not locate where he was coming from.

- We are stray wanderers. We are looking for a place where we could spend the night. Show yourself to us, good lady.

At that moment the door to the cabin slammed shut. The men turned, startled. A girl was already standing at the entrance. It was hard to guess where she suddenly got there.

- Stay. There's a bunk bed over there, you can take it.

The thieves looked at the place she pointed them out. It was completely empty when they entered the cabin, and now there was a bunk bed, nicely made up.

- How is this possible? Pyrlak couldn't believe his eyes. He walked over to the bed to touch it. It was real, solidly made.

- If you are hungry, there is a table in the corner, already set. Please help yourselves. I am going to feed my colorful friends and I will be joining you in a moment.

The girl went outside, and the men stared in disbelief at the small, round table, full of all kinds of hot and cold dishes and drinks. He was not standing in this place when they entered the house, and even now you could smell the delicious food. Hunger prevailed over amazement, and after a while they sat at the table and ate eagerly.

- What now? Seweryn asked.

We'll fill ourselves with it, tie the little one up and throw it into the basement. Easy.

A little butterfly listened to all this conversation. He was sitting on the windowsill with the window open. The men ignored him, and after a while he flew out into the yard to tell the little sorceress what he had heard.

- So that's it! - the girl was indignant - they will learn a lesson! He doesn't mess with me.

After everyone has eaten, it's time to go to sleep. But before the girl got up from the table, the two thieves were already holding her hands.

- Come on. Now you will live in the basement, and we will make ourselves comfortable here forever.

After these words, they took her to the basement and locked the door. When they returned to the living room smug, they were surprised to find the girl standing in front of them.

- What is?! Seweryn shouted.

They repeated the entire operation, but this time they tied a little hand with a rope. But it was to no avail - as soon as they returned from the basement, the girl was standing in front of them again.

- Listen, baby! Pyrlak was angry, "what are these spells?" "My spells!" You'll never hurt me. Now it's my turn to deal the cards.

The hearts of the thieves froze, because suddenly, instead of a sweet girl, a small creature with a wrinkled and deformed face stood before them. Her dry, brown hands, tipped with black claws, hung down to the ground. There were only a few shoulder-length gray hairs on her head. One eye was still closed and saliva was flowing out of the mouth. The creature terrified the men so much that they could not move out of fear.

- Now you will be able to live here forever, but with me as my friends.

At that moment, the creature raised its arms above its ugly head and the whole room filled with a metallic red light. The men felt themselves getting lighter and lighter. Their bodies began to change at an alarming rate, so that after a while they were transformed into two colored butterflies.

"We'll always be together now," said the creature. -If you move away from this house, you will have one day to live. But with me you can live forever ...

The red light was gone and the lovely little girl was standing in the room again.

15. The adventures of little Arthur

There was a little kingdom not so far from here, the king of which adored everything big. It had a great castle with huge walls, and in the castle each room had to have a large area. The royal guards were very tall and each citizen was required to wear long hair. In the town that surrounded the castle, efforts were made to ensure that the collections were plentiful, that the paintings were painted only in the largest format, and so on ...

All residents lived very well here. Only a young man named Arthur had a gloomy life. He was the smallest inhabitant of the city, and since his hair tended to fall out from an early age, he didn't wear it very long. It so happened that once his house was completely burnt down. Neither the king nor any of the inhabitants wanted to help him because he did not fit the canon that the ruler of this kingdom required. Little Arthur was forced to leave his homeland.

- Don't worry, kid - a neighbor consoled him - I have a cousin in a nearby town. Nobody has to be very tall there. All you need is enthusiasm for work. I already told him you were coming. Arthur thanked him and set off on his mare.

The journey did not take long. The neighbor's cousin greeted the boy with open arms.

- I'm glad you're here. It's hard to find a good employee today. People would like to earn, not make money.

- What would I do?

- I am a farmer and I need a harvest assistant. You would also have to take your crops to the market twice a week to sell them. In return, I offer you a place in my stable, food and one silver coin a month.

Arthur agreed to such conditions. He started working the same day. It was hard work, but the bowl of soup prepared by his employer's wife rewarded him.

The days passed peacefully for him, and he finally felt that he had found his place on earth.

One day, the employer called Artur to his place.

- Listen, boy. I have managed to grow a very rare fruit. There is a merchant in the south looking for such specimens. It gives you five gold coins for each seed. Take them and go to him. In return, you will receive one gold coin from me.

The boy was overjoyed. The next day he set off. It had been driving a long time. After a few days, his mare was so tired that she refused to go any further.

- All right, old lady. We will rest for one day and move on. Arthur pitched a tent right next to the river, tied the mare to a tree and went to sleep immediately.

The next day, he noticed with horror that someone had stolen his horse.

- Oh no! How do I get to the merchant now - the boy cried. However, he had no choice but to continue his journey on foot.

After a few days, he reached a large city. It was the first time he had seen so many tall and brick buildings.

"My old king would be speechless with delight," he said to himself.

He was already very tired from the trek, so he headed for the tavern.

Inside it was crowded and stuffy. It was evident that the locals did not have much entertainment. With great effort, he managed to cram into the bar.

"Sorry," he said shyly.

- What? Said rudely a woman who was of considerable size and not of the first youth.

- I'm looking for a room to rent.

- Stranger, right? We rarely host tourists here.

- No, no - the boy chuckled - I'm not a tourist. Rather, I came for a business purpose. I'm bringing a valuable seed for sale. It's worth five gold coins, so you understand that I need to rest before continuing my trek.

Arthur focused on himself the eyes of a few thugs. The barmaid leaned towards him and said:

"Boy, you shouldn't be flaunting such revelations in public." I have a spare room upstairs. I count four silver coins per night, but that's with breakfast! The boy became sad.

- I only have three silver coins. I worked for them for a long time. "Maybe," the woman said, collecting the payment. –This staircase, first floor, second room on the left. You have the key here. - Thank you very much Arthur rejoiced.

He took his bag and headed upstairs. The suspicious type followed right behind him. A man with a very common face with a large number of scars.

The young man entered his room, and as soon as he closed the door behind him, there was a knock.

"Maybe the landlady took pity on me and brought me dinner in addition," he said hopefully to himself, then opened the door. To his surprise, he did not see the dubious beauty of the bartender, and the old man with a knife in his hand. Arthur turned on his heel and ran to the window. It was high enough, but he figured he could escape through it. He didn't have time to open it, however, when he felt a dull pain in the neck area. He became completely foggy, and he fell unconscious to the floor.

He woke up after a few hours. He didn't know what happened. After a while, he remembered the thug who had visited him and stood on his feet. But there was no one in the room. Doors were closed. All Arthur's belongings were scattered around the room.

- The seed! He shouted and reached into his pocket. Unfortunately, there was nothing there. - What am I going to do now! How do I look my employer in the eye? I don't even have anything to come home for ... - The broken boy cried.

He decided to send his hosts a letter describing the whole situation and apologizing to them with all his heart.

- I will not go back there, I have to find a new home.

The evening came, and as the room was bought until the morning, he decided to wash and sleep properly. The next day, he ate a large breakfast, packed what was left of him, and continued on his way. Even though it was a large city, he did not want to look for a new home there. He would always associate this place with thieves.

This time he decided to take the main road in the hope that this way he would avoid another theft. As he was walking for a while, he noticed a few boys by the road. They were standing in a circle and were clearly busy with something. As Arthur approached them, he noticed that the children were abusing an animal.

- Hello! He shouted at them, "go away, leave that animal!" What if someone tormented you so much ?! Get out or I'll talk to your parents!

The boys ran in all directions until they were nowhere to be seen. Arthur ran up to the pet to check if he was okay.

- Owl? He was surprised.

"Yes, the owl..." replied the bird.

- Says? He was surprised again.

- So he says ...

- But…

- Thank you, boy, for saving, - said the owl, dusting off the feathers. -Children can be unbearable.

"Yes," Arthur smiled.

- I noticed that we are going in the same direction. If you want, I could accompany you. For two, it will surely be better for us.

- Of course! I would be honored.

So Arthur and the owl moved on together. Along the way, the bird talked about how it met the cat, which made it want to know the world, and how it had been wandering for a long time.

- Why is this cat not accompanying you anymore? Asked the young man. "I'd rather not talk about it," the owl said shortly.

They spent the rest of their journey in silence. Eventually they came to a great tower with no doors or windows.

- What is it? Asked the bird.

- It's a tower. I just don't know why there are no doors and windows.

They both walked around the building but found nothing. Then the owl saw a small gap between the bricks.

- Can you make it through? Arthur asked.

- I think so - the bird tired of trying to push through the hole for a while, but after a while it was already inside.

- And how?

- It's dark in here. I can see the stairs. I'll go in and see.

Arthur waited a long time for the owl to return. When he called, she did not answer him. Evening came and the boy fell asleep leaning against the tower. The next day the owl still showed no signs of life, and finally the boy began to worry.

- I won't leave her here.

He carefully began to enlarge the hole. He broke off any protruding pieces of brick until the crack was large enough for him to pass through. Unfortunately, during this work, he wiped his hands completely. He started up the stairs that had taken his companion the day before. He walked a long time and he could have sworn that he should have been at the top a long time ago. At last he saw a light in front of him. He entered the chamber and immediately noticed an owl lounging on a large bed.

- What's going on, owl? He exclaimed indignantly. - I've been waiting all night in front of the tower. I thought something happened to you.

- Oh, forgive me, my friend. I've never slept on something so comfortable before. As soon as I lay down, I fell asleep immediately.

Arthur looked around the room. There were no windows, but surely someone lived here, for there were candles everywhere.

- Where's the host?

- I do not know. I haven't seen anyone since I got in here.

"But someone must have lit candles recently," the boy remarked. -But they would burn out overnight.

Suddenly, footsteps could be heard from the stairs. Someone was climbing the mountain. Friends waited anxiously for the arrival of the host, and when he reached the top, they breathed a sigh of relief.

- It's a mouse! Arthur smiled. "It's a mouse ..." the owl licked.

The Mouse stood on two legs and rubbed her eyes in astonishment.

"So you destroyed my entrance to my house," she said reluctantly. - Now anyone can come in. I hope you will make good the damage by leaving!

"Forgive us, dear mouse," said the boy, who was no longer surprised by the talking animals. - We were looking for a shelter.

"You won't find it with me, especially you, the mouse-eater," said the rodent, looking at the owl.

- Of course we apologize for the intrusion. As soon as we go downstairs, I'll fix the entrance. Just tell me one thing, curiosity is eating me up. As far as I know, mice don't build buildings that big. How did you come to live here?

- It's a sad story. A long time ago, a certain queen had a beautiful daughter. All bachelors from the area loved the princess, including a certain young man from the kingdom over the mountain. The beautiful girl reciprocated him and they planned to get married. Unfortunately for them, the queen also had a crush on the young man. Her heart was overcome with anger and jealousy. She decided to get rid of her rival, i.e. her own daughter. Far from the castle, she had a tall tower built without windows. She walled up the princess in it, condemning her to certain death, and she told the young man that his beloved had fled with another. The queen hoped that the boy would want to marry her. But she was wrong. After losing her beloved, the prince threw himself off the cliff, and the queen herself went mad, because she understood that she had lost her beloved man and her beloved daughter at the same time. However, no one knew that the princess lived locked up in this tower for many years. And only because a certain mouse, having found the entrance to the tower, brought the girl water and food. I helped her for a long time. The day finally came when the princess fell asleep forever. And I was left here alone. Since then, I have lived here and look after this place.

"It's a really sad story," Arthur worried. - Forgive us for the incursion.

The boy took the owl under his arm. They said goodbye to the mouse and continued their journey.

They walked in silence for a long time, remembering the story told by the mouse. Their reverie ended as they reached the next stop on their journey.

- Look! The owl shouted. -There's a village there! At last. I am actually starving.

They quickened their pace and in a moment they were there. Unfortunately, it was immediately noticeable that the village was abandoned. All the buildings were literally falling apart. Some buildings were clearly burned down. Only wild chickens were running in the courtyard.

- It's not too bad. We'll have dinner, Arthur said.

In the evening they lit a fire and roasted one of the caught hens. After they had eaten properly, they chose one of the more well-kept houses. They fell asleep deliciously in it. Strange sounds woke them up during the night.

- Arthur, go see what it is - the owl hid under the blanket, so that only its beak protruded.

The boy reluctantly obeyed his companion. He cautiously approached the window and looked out onto the road. It was dark outside. The outlines of the buildings could be seen in the moonlight. The whole city was shrouded in fog. Then just in front of his window a figure flashed like a phantom, without a clear shape. Arthur jumped away from the window. His heart was pounding like crazy.

- Owl. I think it's a ghost town. We have to get out of here.

- But now? The bird scared. - In the middle of the night? This is crazy! Listen to me. If they notice that we are in their area, it may end badly for us.

"A few more hours until dawn," she said pleadingly. –Let's wait.

The boy climbed into his companion under the blanket. Huddled and cuddled to each other, they took refuge in the very corner.

At the same moment, the door swung open. A very strong wind was blowing. Three dark apparitions crawled into the room. They straightened in the middle and as if looked around.

- Are they still here? Are here?

- And they were here? They were?

- If not fools, then with the advent of the night they left.

- Or are they here? I'm hungry.

- And you know who it is? Is it tasty?

- Does not matter! I haven't eaten meat for a long time. I've had enough of hens.

- They slept here. But where are they now?

- They're not here, you can see them.

- We're wasting time. Let's go further.

- Let's go.

- Let's go.

The phantoms flew out, slamming the door behind them. Arthur and the owl remained motionless until dawn. With the sun over the horizon, they quickly packed their things and ran away.

- Let's blow out of here! The owl shouted, flapping its wings at the same time.

Once they were away from the ghostly village, they breathed a sigh of relief.

Several days passed before they reached the next city. It was not big, but the residents took care of it. Everywhere was clean and beautiful flowers bloomed at every house.

"I'm starving," said the bird, patting its belly. "We don't have any money," Arthur worried. - We need to find a job quickly.

Suddenly, a beautifully dressed old man rode into the market square.

- Attention residents! He exclaimed. - The mayor would like to make a communiqué. As we all know, our charming city has been plagued by this nasty monster that lives in a cave behind the forest for years. Giant three-eyed. He eats sheep, kidnaps children, destroys crops. It is high time to deal with this individual. We don't have an army, and the great knights avoid our little town. I hope there are some brave ones among us who will be able to defeat the monster. As a reward, the mayor promises twenty gold coins and the hand of his only daughter.

"This is our chance," Arthur whispered to the owl.

- What are you talking about? She was surprised. "You just ran away from ghosts, and now you want to face a giant?" How do you wanna do this? The boy said nothing to her. He took her arm and headed towards the mayor's house. They were received very friendly on the spot.

"I'm glad you want to help, boy," the mayor began. - We have already lost many men to this monster and I am not surprised by our inhabitants that even a good reward cannot mobilize them to fight. I hope you can handle it.

Before the trip to the cave, the mayor gave some friends food. They also got a good night's sleep in his house. At dawn, they set off to meet the giant.

Upon arriving there, they spotted a cave. They approached cautiously and peered inside.

"It's terrible here," shuddered the owl.

- Hop hop! Arthur shouted, his voice echoed.

- Are you crazy ?! The bird jumped back in horror from the entrance.

Suddenly the ground trembled as if someone were taking very heavy steps. The friends moved away from the cave. After a while, a two-meter-long individual emerged from inside it. It was not a giant, although it did have three eyes. The boy stood in amazement, then said:

- This is a giant? In my home kingdom, such an increase was an absolute minimum!

Only after a while did he notice something he hadn't noticed before. In a small town, all the inhabitants were at least as tall as Arthur. Accustomed to such a height, they decided that this two-meter-tall man is a giant.

- Aren't you afraid of me boy ?! The monster asked thickly.

- Not very. I am not astonished to see you.

- What do you want, kid? You're interrupting my afternoon nap!

- I came on the orders of the mayor. I'm going to end your terror.

The giant laughed mockingly, and then with one move of his hand he pushed Arthur so hard that he flew a few meters. The boy groaned in pain, but stood up and dusted himself off. He ran to the creature and hit it in the stomach with all his strength. This made the giant angry. He hit his opponent with all his might. The blow was so strong that the young man was unable to get up immediately. Seeing this, the owl became furious. It flew to the giant and pecked out two of its eyes. The creature fell to its knees, covering its face with its hands. He was half-blind with one eye. He got up and fled to his pit. In fact, no one has seen him again since then. The bird flew over to its companion and helped him up. Together they returned to the town.

The mayor was very pleased that his guests defeated the harassing giant. He gave a big party in their honor. They also received the promised reward. Arthur met the mayor's daughter and fell in love with her at first sight. She was a miss of considerable beauty and outstanding intelligence.

"Dear friend," said the owl. - I see you've found your place. However, I am already old and I would like to see this and that. Even with your permission, our paths will part now.

- Thank you, dear owl - Arthur was unable to hide his emotion. "If it weren't for you, I wouldn't have been able to get it all.

They hugged each other goodbye. The boy gave the owl fifteen gold coins from the prize, and it continued its journey.

Arthur married the mayor's daughter and they lived happily ever after. He never met an owl again.

16. Sage

In every community there will be a person who in intelligence and life experience surpasses those around him. There was a very old sage in a small village. Nobody remembered how old he was, who his parents were and what he did when he was young. However, each resident at a difficult moment turned to him, asking for good advice.

One day a farmer came to the old man. He was doing badly, very badly. He had no one to hire to help with the harvest. All the men in the village already had jobs and no one applied for him. The old man thought for a moment, then said:

- I know, good man, that fate has gifted you and your wife seven daughters. As far as I remember correctly, five of them are already adults. Not all your girlfriends need to help their mother around the house. Hire them at your place. You will see that women are not only strong and hardworking, but also very accurate.

The farmer heeded the advice of the old man and hired his own children to help. A few weeks later, he visited the sage again. This time he only came to thank him, as - as it turned out - the advice was very accurate.

Another time, a young boy came for help. His parents chose his future wife, and he could not accept it.

- What's the problem, dear boy? The old man asked with interest.

- My master. Thank you for agreeing to receive me. Well, I am to marry the miller's daughter. We are friends and I think he is one of the greatest people I know. Unfortunately, her beauty leaves much to be desired. She is not the type of beautiful maid. I don't want a nasty wife.

- Boy. The matter is very simple. Remember that you would spend your entire life with this person. Beauty will quickly pass, and your friendship and the bond that is between you will remain. And don't worry unnecessarily. If I know your fiancée well, she is still very young and a lot can still happen.

The young man was not too pleased with such advice. The old man, however, was considered a great authority in the village, so he obeyed him and married the miller's daughter. Only years later did he realize that this was the best choice he could make. He fell in love with her, and she herself, feeling loved, blossomed and turned into a real beauty from the ugly duckling.

The house of the sage was on a great hill overlooking the entire valley and the village. Every evening, when no more guests visited him, the old man would sit in the wicker chair in front of the house and watch the sunset. All his days passed in a similar way. He got up in the morning, ate breakfast, and then, practically all day long, he saw "clients". He was a little tired of it, and with time he felt loneliness. The day came when nothing unusual was happening in the village, so no one bothered to seek valuable advice. The old man was a little confused and didn't really know what to do with his free time. He cleaned the house, swept the leaves in the garden, and his ideas ran out. He smiled to himself, thinking that he was so smart and that he couldn't find a job. Eventually, he decided to go to a nearby pond to fish. He couldn't remember the last time he'd done it anymore, but he felt the relaxation would be of use to him.

The fish did not particularly eat that day, but that did not discourage the sage. He enjoyed the peace and quiet. A grunt interrupted his reverie. He turned and saw a boy, about eight years old, next to him.

"Hi," said the little boy.

"Hello," the sage reluctantly greeted the child. He knew he was going to have to deal with other people's problems right now, and he liked the fact that he had a day off.

- What are you doing? The boy came closer and crouched next to the old man.

- I'm resting. I am fishing.

- Yes? I have never caught fish. Could you please teach me?

The old man smiled. He realized that the child had not come especially to him. Apparently it was playing somewhere in the neighborhood.

- I'm not a very good fisherman. My father was one. A real master of fishing!

- Seriously? Will you tell me about him? The boy's eyes sparkled.

He stared at the sage with such pleading eyes that he simply could not refuse him.

- So sit next to me and listen. When I was your age, I spent most of my time at sea with my father. We were using an old fishing boat. What a boat it was! It barely floated. For some reason, my father had a great fondness for her. Even when times were better and he could afford a new boat, he would not buy a new one. Every day before dawn we went out into the open waters. Usually the weather was good for us, but there were also days when we wished we had stayed on land. One day one of the biggest storms took our boat very far from the shore. The sky was overcast and we lost our bearings. With the rest of our strength, we managed to reach a small island. On the spot it turned out that it is not inhabited. I also remember that my father then completely broke down. His boat was useless anymore, it was completely destroyed ...

The old man was silent for a moment and gazed thoughtfully at the surface of the water.

- And what? The boy asked impatiently. - Did you get off the island?

- Rather yes - the wise man winked with a smile - since I'm here today and talking to you.

The child blushed and fell silent.

- Ha, ha! Don't worry, he patted the boy on the shoulder as he spoke. - I'd love to tell you what happened next. But now you should be going home. It's late and your parents are sure to be worried about you.

- Let's meet in a week and I'll finish this story for you.

The little boy nodded, said goodbye, and ran towards the village.

From then on, they met regularly by the pond. The sage taught his little friend to fish and told him various stories from his extremely long life. He wasn't lonely anymore. He found a companion.

17. The monster from under the bed

A long time ago, in a nice house, there lived a mother with a little daughter. The girl's name was Nadia. She was a tiny blonde with blue eyes. Everyone in the neighborhood was delighted with her and congratulated the mother on such a lovely baby.

As the girl grew, she had more and more responsibilities at home. The most important of these was keeping your room in order.

- Remember to clean up toys after each play - mom used to say - you are already old enough that I will not do it for you. - Good, good - replied the buckthorn.

The whole girl's room was filled to the brim with all kinds of teddy bears, stuffed bunnies, beautiful dolls and wooden blocks. The little one loved to play with it all and often lost track of time.

"It's time to sleep," my mother called from the kitchen.

- Oh no - the girl saddened as she looked around the room - a terrible mess here, and after a whole day of fun, I have no strength for anything. It's best to leave it there and clean it up in the morning when I'm asleep. So she did. The next day, when mom entered her daughter's room, she called out:

- Nadia! What is this terrible mess?

The girl woke up immediately.

- Mom, forgive me. It will not happen again. I promise to clean up after myself forever.

Mom took the child's word for it. However, the situation repeated itself notoriously.

- Listen, little daughter. If you don't keep your room tidy, a monster will breed under your bed! You don't want this, do you?

Nadia shook her head. She started cleaning up quickly. But as she began to sort her toys, she found a few that she had long forgotten existed. She was so happy about it that she immediately started playing. Time passed very quickly, and it was evening before she knew it.

- Oh no! She said to herself. -That mess again. I'll clean up tomorrow. After all, nothing will happen.

The next day, as soon as the girl woke up, she noticed something surprising. The floor of the room was completely empty! There was not a single toy lying there. Nadia quickly ran to her mother.

- Mom, mom! Thank you for cleaning my room last night. I promise that from now on I will always clean up everything myself. - What a baby! My mother was surprised. - What are you talking about? I didn't clean up anything for you.

The girl returned to the room. She checked the cupboards, trunk, and shelves. The toys she had been playing with the night before were nowhere to be found.

"Well," she said. - Apparently my mother wants to teach me a lesson.

On the same day, Nadia, as usual, gave herself to play. But she didn't clean up after herself this time. Also this time, the toys left on the floor are gone. The situation repeated until the girl was left with not a single toy except for the cuddly kitten she was sleeping with. The girl was very much grieved at the loss of her beloved toys.

"I told you," my mother said. –I did. The tears will be useless now.

That night, little Nadia could not sleep. She hugged her soft toy with all her strength, because she was afraid that she might also lose him. Suddenly a shadow crept from under the bed. The girl froze with fear and held her breath. Terrible paws with huge claws emerged just behind the shadow. The monstrous hands felt carefully at the floor next to the bed. But when they missed nothing, there was a groan:

- Hey! Where are the toys! The voice was terrible, hoarse and very thick. -What am I supposed to eat now? I'm hungry!

After these words, the hands extended even more, and behind them the whole thing emerged. It was dark as night. He had large, bulging white eyes that were entirely veined with red. He looked around and saw little Nadia covered with a blanket up to her nose.

- What do we have here? The monster said with satisfaction. - A little starter!

The girl screamed. As soon as the creature began to approach her, she threw her plush kitty at it. The monster grabbed the toy and said:

- But fluffy! You are lucky little girl. This will satisfy my hunger, but tomorrow I will definitely come back for you.

The bogeyman swallowed the stuffed animal at once, then disappeared back under the bed. Terrified Nadia ran out of the room and, screaming ravily, went to her mother's bedroom.

- What's wrong, baby? The woman asked anxiously.

The girl told her the whole story.

- Oh not good! Mom worried. - I don't know what we can do. Let's clean the whole house. Maybe it will help.

So they did. They both cleaned every corner of the apartment, wiped the chicken, collected papers, even the tableware was polished. When night fell, Nadia and her mother waited in the kitchen for the monster to come. Suddenly, footsteps could be heard from behind the door to the children's room. Something was rummaging around the room. We could hear the opening and closing of cabinets, drawers and the shuffling of a chair.

- We have to smoke him out of here - Mom carefully approached the door from the room. - You stay here.

Nadia nodded and hid behind the kitchen cupboard.

When mom entered her daughter's room, she saw the creature in the middle. He was looking for something to eat in vain. After a while, however, he caught the man's presence. He turned and when he saw my mother he said:

- It's a bit big ... I only eat toys, rubbish or even children ...

"Get out, monster, from our house!" Mom shouted. Unfortunately, the creature only laughed mockingly and went back to searching the room. Mother's pleas and threats were useless. The monster had settled in for good, and there was no way it was going to leave. You had to find a new home as soon as possible. The next day, Nadia and her mother moved to another building - on the other side of town. From then on, the girl always cleaned up after herself and took care of her toys. Thanks to this, she never met the monster from under the bed again.

18. Pink lock

In a great castle in the highlands lived a royal family: king, queen and little princess. Princess Victoria was the apple of her parents' eye. They fulfilled her every whim and allowed her to do anything.

The color of pink in the world was the favorite of the princess. So she had pink dresses, shoes, every piece of furniture in her room, and sheets. Even at her request, the king ordered extremely rare and expensive pink candles to be brought. She did not accept clothes or even gifts of a different color.

There was no end to Victoria's caprices. It got to the point that she even ordered horses throughout the kingdom to be dyed in her favorite color. The other inhabitants didn't like it all, but they had to fulfill her wishes. The king made sure that no one ever opposed his daughter. Until one day, during a joint dinner, the princess announced:

- I wish that our entire castle would be pink on the outside.

The king and queen looked at each other. They both thought it was too much. Unfortunately, each of their refusals ended in a monstrous scream and cry of the princess, so this time they agreed to her request. All the men in the castle painted its walls for several days. When they finished, the princess was thrilled. It was a dream come true for her. She thanked her parents with all her heart. But it was noticeable that she was the only one who enjoyed this drastic change. The inhabitants were afraid that now the surrounding kingdoms would not take them seriously, not to mention the fact that their eyes ached just looking at the walls.

All this was watched by the witch from her treehouse on the hill, directly opposite the pink castle.

- What's that supposed to mean? She was saying to herself. - Is it still a kingdom or is it already a kindergarten? I feel sick looking at this color… I have to do something about it.

The witch did not sleep all night. Finally she figured out what to do.

The next day the witch, disguised as an old shepherdess, went to the castle. Right next to its walls, she met a princess playing with a pink poodle.

"Hello, little girl," she said.

- Hello, old lady. What brings you to our kingdom?

- Well, my child, in my hometown it is not as joyful as it is here. So I collect colorful things to bring some colors to my home.

- I'll help you. I know colors like hardly anyone - Wiktoria replied coquettishly.

The princess ran to the poodle and pulled out some of its pink hair. Then she went in search of other colors and after a while she brought the old woman a whole bag of all kinds of things: blue beads, red ribbons, green cufflinks, yellow fabrics and much more.

- Thank you, sweetheart. The old woman took the bag and turned back to her side. And the farther she moved away from the castle, the paler all the colors that surrounded it became. Finally, when the shepherdess disappeared from the eyes of the princess, it turned out that she had taken all the colors with her. The castle, its surroundings and all inhabitants became black and white.

Princess Victoria cried out loud. How will she live without colors now? There are no pink walls anymore, her dress does not sparkle with a rainbow, and there was a completely white poodle standing next to it.

The King and Queen quickly noticed this change. They asked the guards and the ladies of the court, but no one could tell them how it could have happened. Only the princess stood silently beside her.

During the next few days, all the inhabitants of the castle became very sad. Along with the colors, they lost the will to live. Now even the flowers didn't want to smell, and the food didn't seem to have any taste. When in the evening Princess Victoria brushed her hair before going to bed, she cried aloud:

- Oh. Life without colors is so sad. I wish I had appreciated the other colors. I miss the yellow sun and red roses. I miss my mom's burgundy dress and my dad's navy blue coat. I would like to see once again how beautiful pheasants and peacocks are. And now everything around is black and white, gray, lifeless!

The princess hid her face in her hands. Tears were running down her cheeks. She grabbed her handkerchief, once all pink, with gold ornaments, and now completely gray. She wiped her face thoroughly, then went to sleep.

Meanwhile, the king and his wife were trying to find out where all the colors had gone.

"We've literally questioned everyone," said the king. - Nobody saw anything.

- Dear husband. Maybe Wiktoria knows something. After all, she ruled the colors throughout the kingdom.

- You're right. We haven't talked to her yet. Go to her, honey. The Queen went to the princess's chamber and knocked, and when she heard no answer, she looked inside. The princess was already asleep.

- Wake up, little daughter.

- Mom? The princess wiped her eyes swollen with tears.

- It's me. Tell me baby, do you know where all the colors have gone?

The girl told what happened. At the same time, she cried a lot.

- You see, my child. It was a witch living next door. Apparently she couldn't take your antics anymore. Now go to her and get our colors back.

Victoria reluctantly but obeyed her mother and the next day headed for the treehouse.

Once she was there, she picked up a small stone and threw it at the window.

- Who's there? The old woman looked.

"It's me ... Princess Victoria." I would like to ask you to give us our colors.

- There is no speech! The witch was indignant. - I couldn't look at that rose of yours anymore! Do you consider others at all, child? Do you take my opinion into account? Because you don't take the opinion of your parents and your subordinates into account, we already know that.

Victoria lowered her head. She realized that she shouldn't force others to have the same tastes and preferences as she did.

"I'm very sorry," she said finally. - I promise that I will no longer order others to like what I do. Will you give us the colors now.

- You can choose one color. Let me guess ... pink?

- No ... Blue, please, or not - yellow ... Maybe red is better.

- You can see it! The witch laughed. –You can't make it just one color. All are needed!

The witch hid in the tree house and the princess after a while doubted that the witch would give back what she had taken. As she turned on her heel to return to the castle, she heard something fall to the ground behind her. It was a bag with all the things the princess had given the old shepherdess.

- Thank you very much! The girl shouted, grabbing the bag. With all her strength, she ran to the castle, and the closer she was to it, the more it became saturated with colors. After a while, everything was as before. All the colors returned, and the castle was completely covered in pink.

- You did it! - the queen hugged her daughter tightly - are you surely glad that you got your lock back?

- Not really, mom. I'm glad, but I understood that each thing has its own color. I will not impose my style on others. My colors will only be valid in my room. Let's paint the lock back.

The King and Queen were overjoyed to hear this. This time, everyone started painting, including Princess Victoria. And so the castle became gray and ordinary again, but under a blue sky, surrounded by green grass and beautiful, colorful flowers.

19. Two-headed monster

In a world where all kinds of creatures, leprechauns, fairies and other magical creatures lived, there was also a certain monster. However, he was not an ordinary monster as he had two heads. Each of them had their own view of the world, their favorite flavor or color. The right head was very lazy. She didn't feel like traveling or working. She liked to lie down and look at the clouds the most.

The left head, on the other hand, had only active ideas. She liked to climb, penetrate caves and look for beautiful queens.

The heads, due to their differences, kept arguing among themselves what the monster was supposed to do at any given moment.

- It's raining. It will be best if we stay at home today - said a lazy head once.

- Are you kidding ?! - answered the other. - All the people hid in their houses. Let's go to one village and take a house with the whole family! There will be something to eat.

- No way! Because of your carrying of houses, only my cross hurts!

"You are so lazy," the active head irritated. - You can't sleep your whole life. To have something, you have to work hard.

And so, day after day, one monster fought fiercely against itself. The disagreements caused him so much stress that he developed abdominal pain. Of course, this was another reason for polemics. The right head claimed that the pain was caused by a poor diet, fast and ill-considered eating. The other, on the other hand, believed that it was all due to a lack of exercise. In a way, they were both right, but they couldn't find a middle ground.

One day, a young mage was walking next to the monster's cavity. Hearing an argument, he decided to look inside.

- What is going on here? The amazed young man asked. - Why are you arguing so? Hear you at the other end of the forest.

- And you see, wanderer - began the left head - all the fault of this lazy. Because of him, I am unable to spread my wings.

"It's not my fault you have crazy ideas," said the lazy monster. - I'm too fragile to keep up with you.

The mage felt sorry for the creature, which lived in constant tension. He wanted to help him, but his skills weren't yet big enough to deal with the whole thing. Finally, he stated:

"I'd love to help you, but I'm just a beginner wizard." I'm on my way to city A. There are many experienced and powerful magicians there. Perhaps one of them will be able to advise you.

This time both heads were completely in agreement. So they set off together towards the city.

The road wasn't long, but the monster's constant bickering meant that, instead of in one day, they only got there after three days.

"Finally," the young man breathed, seeing the walls. - It may surprise you, but I also find it hard to bear with you.

As soon as they were in town A, the young mage immediately led them to his master's hut.

The old man was sitting in the big armchair and he looked as if he were only waiting for them to come. The monster quickly presented his problem, and the old mage soon had a solution:

- Nature made you that way. There are two options: you will either accept yourself and the differences that are between you, or I will have to amputate one of you.

The heads looked at each other. This was not the answer they expected. Now would they decide which one would stay? Only one? Will they never see each other again? It wouldn't be a good choice.

"So yes," the lazy head began, "this is my brother, part of me." Even if we don't get along, I can't pass a death sentence on him.

"I feel the same," said the rights. "I couldn't have him amputated."

The old man nodded understandingly.

- Get out, monster. I'd like to talk to the young man who brought you to me. I think there is another way to help you. The monster obediently went outside. At that time, the old magician turned to the boy:

- There is a valley beyond the Big Mountain. A tree of great power grows there. It only takes a few leaves to separate the two. If you want to help them, go over there and bring me a handful of these leaves.

The young mage and the monster set out in search of the magic tree. Surprisingly, during this trip, both heads were exceptionally unanimous. After a few days, they stood at the foot of Wielka Góra.

"A lot," the right head noted. - I'm all for a break before climbing.

His companions agreed to such an offer and decided to leave in the morning as soon as they had a good night's sleep.

The climbing was not easy. This mountain was very inaccessible. Rocks crumbled and fell easily. The damage left by frequent avalanches was visible everywhere. Over one of the bluffs, the monster slipped and slipped. He only saved himself from falling down because he grabbed a protruding root.

- You see! The left head shouted. - If we exercised more often, I would be able to draw us in, and this is how we will be killed. - Take care! The magician shouted. - I'll get you out right now!

The boy raised the staff he was holding in his hand and uttered a few words incomprehensible to the monster. After a while, the root protruding from the rock moved. He moved even farther and wrapped the monster around his waist. He pulled it with great ease onto the road, then hid it back into the rock. The monster breathed a sigh of relief and thanked his young savior. They started on their way carefully, carefully checking the stability of the road.

Several days passed before they saw a great green valley. In its center stood a huge tree, the size of a huge castle.

"Quite a lot," the right head remarked again. - Before we climb them, I suggest you rest a bit.

And this time they all agreed to it. After a short nap, they walked towards the tree. The leaves were several dozen meters high.

- And what now? The left head asked.

"I don't know," the magician mused.

"Can't you make the tree move again and hand us the leaves by itself."

"It's too big," the boy thought aloud. - I can't make it. But he will try to climb.

As he said, so did he. He carefully grasped the trunk with both hands and began to climb. After a few minutes, he managed to reach the first branch. With an efficient movement of one hand, he broke off a dozen or so leaves and put them in a purse. Slowly he began to descend. Unfortunately, he quickly lost his balance and fell down. The monster showed reflexes, however, and before the boy fell to the ground, he caught him. Satisfied comrades set off on their way back to town A. There the old man was waiting for them.

- I can see you've made it. Pass me the leaves, boy.

The young man gave his master a purse. He took out a few leaves and threw them into a previously prepared pot. After a while, the broth was ready. The old man handed the boy a bottle.

- Come back to their house with them. Let them drink half of them before going to bed. In the morning they should be satisfied with the results.
The boy and the monster returned to the cave. Both heads took their part of the infusion just before going to sleep, and then fell asleep in a rocky sleep. Throughout the night, the young magician watched over his friend. In the morning, the dream felt cold and his eyelids. A scream woke him. The mage got to his feet.
- What happened?! He exclaimed in horror.
- Look! The heads shouted simultaneously. There was no longer a two-headed monster in front of the boy, but two separate monsters of similar stature. Their joy was endless. They jumped, hugged and danced. Finally, quarrels and disagreements will end. After all, each of them could do what they liked. And so the active monster jumped to the young magician in an instant. He was very agile and fast. Before the boy knew it, he was already being held by an old friend. In one move, the monster swallowed the young man.
The moral is that you shouldn't help the monsters that eat people.

THE END

www.ingramcontent.com/pod-product-compliance
Lightning Source LLC
LaVergne TN
LVHW050337160826
845677LV00014B/3660